THAT CLOUD
LOOKS
LIKE JESUS

THAT CLOUD LOOKS LIKE JESUS

...Plus 53 Other
Strange, Bizarre
(and Possibly True)
Stories You'll Never
See in the
New York Times

Marc Berlin

A B B BOOK

Photo newspaper illustrations by Carol Healy and Marc Berlin
Interior book design by David Moratto

Library of Congress Control Number: 2012913493

ISBN: 978-0-9859624-0-1

To Heidi

Disclaimer

Foreword

Many interesting news items which first appear in local newspapers never make it into the national press, and are usually all but forgotten. The following incredible, and possibly true news stories were discovered in various small town journals across the USA, and compiled within these pages for the reader's enjoyment.

Man Talks on Phone to Dictator

WEBB FINNEL, 38, of Kelp Sands, Florida, telephoned his elderly mother to wish her a happy birthday, but got connected to the offices of North Korean leader Kim Jong Il by mistake. Finnel says he spoke to the "Dear Leader" for "maybe a couple of minutes" before he had to abruptly end the call and pick up his girlfriend at the laundromat. "Other than the screaming in the background, he seemed like a nice guy," Finnel said.

Teenager Misses Manhole By Inches

By Bill Schweppler

SNYDE VERREL, 16, a Grillman High School student, narrowly missed falling into a manhole near his home late Friday night. Verrel admitted he'd been daydreaming, ironically, "about what it must be like to fall into a manhole."

BABY BOARDS PLANE TO ASIA

BETHENY REEDLER, a single mother in Plennum, Utah, became hysterical after learning her year-old baby girl, Amanda, had seconds before "just walked away" from their home one evening. The girl was found by police thirteen hours later, checking into a budget motel in Nagoya, Japan. "Except for some jet lag, she's completely OK," Reedler said.

Insect Gives "Speech" on Patio

By Kim Busby

A TINY WOOD mite traversing Roger Flegg's backyard deck started reciting Mark Antony's famous 'Bury Caesar' speech from Shakespeare's "Julius Caesar" before Flegg "got really nervous" and squashed it flat with his shoe. "I've never liked Shakespeare," Flegg said, "but now I'm reading all his plays. The sonnets, too.

gone for good.

Man Finds Dollar in Dispose-all

DEL CREEMER, 19, a hardware clerk in Falls Church, Virgina, was rinsing dishes in his parents' kitchen when he discovered a dollar bill in the dispose-all. After holding onto the loot for a few weeks, Creemer finally turned the money in to police. "I felt guilty," Creemer said. "It wasn't mine to keep.

ιhan, ͻ͵

Backyard Tree Starts Crying

An oak tree in Thad Johnson's yard in Bellevue, Washington, after exposure to pesticides earlier in the day, began "crying like a baby." "If you looked real close you could see the tears", Johnson said. "I guess maybe it was sad for some reason." "We got some weeping willows back there too," Johnson's wife, Kitty, said. "They're real depressed."

CLOUD LOOKS LIKE JESUS

KESTER HUB-BLE, 52, of Mallard, Wyoming, was taking photos of the sky, when he snapped a cloud that looked, according to Hubble, "a lot like Jesus." An avid amateur photographer, Hubble said the cloud evaporated soon afterwards, reappeared once again, "then was gone for good."

CRICKET SOUNDS LIKE ELVIS

A cricket in Frank Kippy 's bushes sounded, according to Kippy, remarkably like Elvis Presley. Kippy, 53, of Drudge Harbor, Massachusetts, later tried to capture the insect, but couldn't find it after searching for several hours. "I think it was singing 'Don't Be Cruel' when I first heard him," Kippy said. "It had a damn good voice, that bug," he added. "Damn good."

Hand Lives After Man Dies

BY FLOYD JOHNSON

A MAN who died in a head-on collision on Interstate 10 near Jiffy started moving suddenly, after "technically" being dead for three hours. Morgue employee, Joe Flence, 26, a Stinkley resident, witnessed the bizarre incident. "That hand — it was definitely moving," Flence said. "I think it gave me the finger."

 on, needier said.

CAR GETS "MAD" AT OWNER

APRIL GISHKIS, 44, of Guppy Hills, California had just left her car, when the vehicle's horn started honking repeatedly, as if it were angry it had to sit alone in the driveway. "I think maybe it was just thirsty, you know, for gas, or oil," Gishkis said. The automobile started up later without a problem.

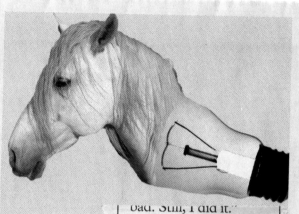

bad. Still, I did it."

Light Bulb Imitates TV Character

A light bulb in Patty Forrester's den in Dodge City, Kansas, started "talking" like the TV horse Mr. Ed for several minutes. When she turned out the light, "the talking stopped, just like that," Forrester said. Forrester also owns a cuckoo clock that chirps like George W. Bush, and a dishwasher that drones like Bill Clinton.

Grandmother Uncovers "City" in Back Yard

By Val MacAdam

LETTY GIPPERS, 84, a Crisco resident, accidentally discovered a miniature buried "city" while digging near her tomato garden behind her home. The "city" had actual streets, buildings, a working police station and even a school. After telling her husband about her discovery, the couple carefully re-covered the tiny metropolis with dirt. "It's a mystery," Gippers said. "A whole little city, in my own back yard."

"It's a mystery, a whole little city, in my own back yard."

CLIP HOLDER QUOTES EX-PRESIDENT

A smiley face magnetic paper clip holder on Reg Arnold's office desk in Homer, Wisconsin, started quoting the 41st president, George H.W. Bush, during Arnold's lunch break. Other workers heard it too, and were "freaking out" for several minutes before help arrived. "I thought they were kidding," Al Budge, 46, the office manager, said. "Then I heard it myself, with my own ears."

"READ MY LIPS..."

Toddler Solves World Problems

By Bill Leppers

A four-year-old boy shocked his parents and extended family in Jugg-man Saturday afternoon when he offered a concise, well thought out plan for solving the world's problems. The toddler, Kevin Carnahan, suddenly told his family during a mid-summer barbecue that he had a plan to solve "all the world's major problems," just before he bit into a hot dog, then jumped into the family's swimming pool. The boy "splashed around for several minutes," then couldn't remember any of what he'd said.

MAN TRAVELS WITH ALIENS ON LUNCH BREAK

"ALIENS" in the executive washroom confronted a man on his lunch break in Plano, Utah. Spence Fumbler, 34, claims he "agreed to travel" with the aliens, as long as he'd be back in time for an afternoon meeting. Fumbler said he was soon travelling "in some weird sixth dimension, maybe near Mercury," then brought back as agreed, just minutes before his meeting.

Picasso Found in Swimming Pool

A man cleaning his swimming pool discovered a rare Picasso painting which had long been thought lost. Judd Eggers, 48, of Carlsbad, Nevada, was cleaning his backyard pool when the Picasso suddenly floated to the surface, then stayed there until Eggers could retrieve it. Eggers turned the masterpiece into police a week later, "after letting it hang in my garage for a while."

WOMAN CRAWLS TO RUSSIA

JESSE GENTNER, 24, of Custer, Montana, had always dreamed of being in the Guinness Book of World Records, by doing what she does best—crawling. Sick of waiting, Gentner got down on her knees, then crawled 6,326 miles, with stops for food and sleep, from her home in Custer to Vladivostok, Russia. The trip, which included crawls across the Bering Sea, then down the Kamchatka Peninsula, took eight months and four days to complete, but got Gentner her well-earned place in Guinness's famous book. "My knees are killing me," she said. "Still, I'm in that damned book."

Man Proposes to Own Mother

By Wilbur Noonan

A man who returned drunk from a night out with his girlfriend accidentally proposed the same night — to his mother. Will Grimm, 33, of East Held, was too drunk to notice he was talking to his mother later the same night, instead of his girlfriend. His mother Emma, 74, declined the proposal, telling her son she was "already happily married."

John Doe
123 Main Street
Anytown, USA 01234

SPUTUM MAN GETS SECRETS FROM PENTAGON

A MAN OPENED his mail to discover he'd accidentally received top secret, highly classified nuclear launch codes mailed to him from the Pentagon. "I think they were meant for the President," Judd Wister, 55, of Sputum, Oregon later explained to a government investigator. "I read the stuff but, I guess luckily, it was all mumbo jumbo."

and top hat only a...   8 ..times... store ma.

COP ARRESTS SELF ON HIGHWAY

BY SWINK MULDOON

A 22-year veteran of the North Smudge police force, Harve Kinnard, 43, arrested himself after driving erratically following a family Christmas party early Wednesday morning. Kinnard pulled into the breakdown lane, handcuffed himself, and then called a friend who drove him to the police station, three miles away. "Don't drink and drive," Kinnard said later. "It isn't worth getting arrested, even by yourself."

R

"V

Man Writes Book — While Sleeping

A retired schoolteacher who sleepwalks nightly completed a 275-page economics textbook he'd begun in 1989. Kyle Riffler, 63, of Sturgeon Bay Wisconsin, finally finished his opus after a long nap at his brother's house New Year's Day. "My husband's most creative while asleep," Riffler's wife Betty, said. "While awake, he can't tie his own shoes."

Man is Friends With Fence

By Marty Swinkmeyer

FRED BUTTMAN, 29, a Festus Groves resident, is "friends" with a sixty-foot wooden fence near his home. Several years ago, the fence started creaking loudly each time Buttman passed it on his way to work as a poultry inspector, until now Buttman completely understands everything the barrier is saying. "I think it understands me, too," Buttman said. "I hope so."

GIRL GETS CRUMB FROM GOVERNOR

TESSIE POTTER, 14, of Flounder Bay, Massachusetts, is a huge fan of her own Governor, Mitt Romney. She even sent him a fan letter. So when Potter received a letter back, she was ecstatic. She opened the letter to discover the Governor had sent her a tiny crumb of food. "Here's something to remember me by," Romney wrote on official stationery the single brown crumb came wrapped in. "He's still a good guy," Tessie said. "And tall, too."

LOBSTER BEGS FOR LIFE

A five-pound giant lobster "begged" for its life after being caught by a Maine lobsterman. Kirby Dreggs, 40, of Seafood, Maine, trapped the crustacean, then distinctly heard it "screaming and begging" for its life as he hauled it aboard his trawler, The Rusty Claw. Dreggs said he consoled the creature "for maybe ten minutes," then tossed it back.

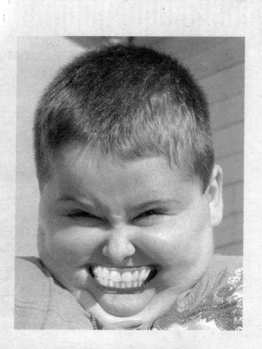

Boy Expelled For Smiling

BY FINK HARLOWE

An eight-year-old fourth grader, Shelby Stickle, was expelled from the John Wilkes Booth Memorial Elementary School in Fudgeton last Thursday when a teacher thought he was "smiling too much." The teacher, Reed Flenk, told school committee members the boy was always smiling, "even after I told him to stop. It was torture." Flenk, 49, was put on administrative leave pending an investigation.

Man Embezzles 50 Cents to Pay Meter

A MAN SHORT fifty cents to pay a parking meter resorted to larceny to get the money. Hal "Red" Kribbs, 39, of Mosquito, Florida, said he'd found the perfect spot to park for the day, but had no change for the meter. "I went up to my office, fiddled with the books, then took the money out of petty cash," Kribbs said. "I feel awfully awfully bad. Still, I did it."

MAN GETS 25 YEARS FOR STEALING PIE

Connorsville — A Georgia man, Pike Lawson, 55, was sentenced Tuesday to 25 years in state prison for stealing a blueberry pie from a neighbor's porch. The judge hearing the case, Hank "Gator" Phelps, said the harsh sentence was justified as Lawson had stolen before. "This was his second offense," Phelps explained. "He stole some bread last February."

PONY SCRIBES BOOK BY TAPPING

By Megan Krinkle

A TWO-YEAR-OLD Shetland pony belonging to Trudy Mulch, 15, of Cleftburg, has written a two-hundred-page book — by tapping the words out with her hoof. "She taps almost every day, between nine and two, out in the barn," Trudy explained. "I write it all down by hand, then type it later." The book, entitled "Hegel, Marx, and the Rise of Industrial England," will be available at local bookstores starting in May.

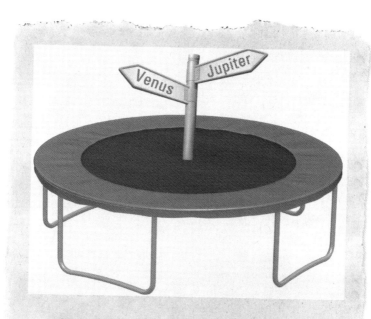

MAN USES TRAMPOLINE TO EXPLORE SOLAR SYSTEM

A man uses a backyard trampoline to bounce his way into the heavens. Floyd Dent, 31, of Gull, Mississippi, is an expert on the trampoline. Dent says he routinely catapults himself to distant planets, simply by bouncing on his trampoline. "It's a handy little contraption," Dent says. "I can go anywhere I want, right here on earth, too. I save a ton on airfare."

Family Lives in Shoebox

BY DEL CRUIKSHANK

A family evicted from their apartment has been living in a size 11 shoebox off Interstate 15. Hank Mueller, 27, his wife Sabrina and their seven children were forced out of their apartment in July after Mueller was laid off from his job as a night watchman. "We walked around homeless for maybe forty days, until, luckily, we found this shoebox," Mueller explained. He added: "It's a tight fit, but it works. We'll be OK as long as no one moves."

MAN IS PRESIDENT — FOR TWO MINUTES

By Clem "Pinch" McCabe

A Stillsby man who'd drifted away from a White House tour accidentally found himself in a very special place. After walking around "clearly lost" for a while, the man ended up in the Oval Office, by himself. "I sat at the desk and pretended to be president," Orville Shrub, 46, told a Secret Service agent afterwards. "I called the IRS, then the Pentagon, finally the CIA before I got a little bored." Shrub found his way back to his tour group, then had lunch.

Mom Orders Pizza, Gets Tractor

A MOM ORDERING pizza for her three kids got a lot more than she bargained for. On August 24, Tracy Stenk of Vole, Iowa ordered a large mushroom pizza from a local pizzeria. "Two hours later, this fellow showed up with a three-ton utility tractor," Stenk said. "He said I ordered it, but I didn't." The snafu occurred when Stenk's pizzeria call was accidentally re-routed to a John Deere sales office in Minneapolis. "The salesperson thought she wanted a tractor," a spokesman for Deere later said. "Her credit checked out. We gave her what she wanted."

LINCOLN RELATIVE ARRESTED FOR LOITERING

A distant relative of Abraham Lincoln was arrested outside a Hibbing, Illinois Wal-Mart for loitering and trespass. According to police, Ron Lincoln, a great great grandnephew of the 16 th president, was first noticed by Wal-Mart management late Thursday night. "He was definitely loitering, so I called the cops," Errol Scrubbs, 58, the store manager said. "He had this thick beard and top hat on, and was talking to himself. He looked real suspicious."

Oregon Man Losing Home — From Overdue Book

By Lloyd Frisbee III

HANK ESTES, 70, a retired pipefitter, was informed by Seaside Public Library officials last Wednesday that he owed $219,009 in accumulated fines for a book he'd taken out 30 years earlier. "I'm about to lose my home over this," Estes said after a court hearing. "It's really unfair." The book in question is called, "Get Rich and Stay That Way". "That's the craziest part," Estes said.

...ss the
I really will."

Capital City Man Arrested for Whispering

A man withdrawing money from a bank was arrested Saturday afternoon — for whispering. Floyd Kegler, 48, of Capital City, Nebraska, was arrested after a teller noticed Kegler was whispering his request to withdraw seventy-five dollars from his own account. "I thought he was a robber," the teller said. Kegler explained: "I was whispering because I'd just had throat surgery. My voice was gone." Kegler was released an hour later, and advised by police to speak up, "especially in banks."

PILOT LANDS ON HORSE

A Lufton, Tennessee man landed his light airplane on a horse Wednesday afternoon, successfully. Creed Fillmore, 51, was heading home from out of state when his Cessna Skyhawk ran out of fuel, forcing him to make an emergency landing in a cornfield. "The field was all dug up, but then I saw this horse running," Fillmore said. "So I aimed best I could, and landed — on him."

Twins Hate Each Other

SALLY AND SUSIE Pillard, of Phlegm, Iowa are a rarity— identical twins. Yet, after thirty-five years together, they hate each other. "It's weird," Susie said, talking about Sally. "We're exactly the same in every way, but for some reason everything she does annoys me. I hate even thinking about her. We stopped talking three months ago." Her sister feels exactly the same way.

OSWEGO MAN BULLIED BY BIRD

AN OSWEGO, New York man says he's been bullied numerous times over three weeks by a wild bird, and he's sick of it. Edgar Flice, 72, says the bird, a large black raven, will hover over him, crow loudly for several minutes, then fly away, "but only if I give him my lunch first." According to Flice, the bird has made him miserable. "I'm getting real depressed," he said. "If it goes on much longer, I'll kill myself."

PET IS STAND-UP COMIC

By John J. Johnson III

Lindsay and Vern Holloway, longtime Cremley residents, have a special dog, a beagle named Chowder. Like most pets, Chowder can run, sit and even retrieve. But Chowder is very unique, in that he also performs standup comedy. "It's crazy," Vern explains. "Every Saturday night like clockwork, he gets up on his hind legs, and does a whole routine in the den. Politics, sports, any topic you can think of, he covers it. The first time I heard him, I fell off the sofa."

Boy Runs Away, To Own Home

BY BUNK STENNIS

A SOUTH WHISTLER boy ran away from home Thursday night — to his own home. "I was really bored, and feeling useless, so I ran away," Rufus Crimp, 15, explained to police. "But then I got lost in the dark, and somehow ended up back where I started — at my own house." The boy was slightly shaken. But mostly, he was embarrassed. "He feels kind of stupid," his father said. "Worse than when he ran away."

Family Trapped by Glue

A family living near a glue factory was imprisoned suddenly by a river of it, glue, that is. Pope Fillard, 59, of Blister, Texas, said his family was trapped in their trailer home when a torrent of airplane glue cascaded over a nearby hill, spilling into their front lawn. "It came in real fast. There was no time to escape," Fillard said. "It got real sticky there for a while," he said. "Real sticky."

SHOE WINS LOTTERY

MARV ZIPPERS of Plankton, Washington likes to play the Lottery. But when he left his wallet at home one night, he had no way to pay. "I felt bad for the guy, so I let him pay with his shoe, a loafer," Ferde Cubby, 28, the store clerk who sold the ticket, said. "He came in the next morning to claim a prize — $500." State lottery officials say no other person has ever won paying with a shoe. "Or any other item of clothing."

Girl Wakes up in Casket

By Stib Dupre

A 14-year old Filmer girl woke up terrified Thursday afternoon after spending the night laying in a casket. Wilk Kippy was visiting Prell's Funeral Home on a school field trip, when she accidentally hit her head and fell into an open casket. The same casket was used later that day for a funeral. "We heard her crying and dug her up," a cemetery employee, Bing Triplett recalled. "Now I know what it's like being dead," Kippy said. "Believe me, alive's a lot better."

WOMAN *"EXPLODES"* AT PARTY

A WOMAN already seriously overweight "blew up" after eating too much cake at a family reunion. Kilt "Bib" Hopper, 52, of Leavenworth, Kansas, had just finished dessert at a family reunion when her stomach burst, showering partly digested food over many of the other guests. "She was headed for the buffet table for more pie when it happened," Stub Buford, 65, a relative, said. "She exploded. That's all you can say." Hopper was rushed to a local hospital, and will survive.

Girl Wakes up in Casket

Girl "Too Pretty" For School

BY LES MILDEW

A Bilge student was removed from class Wednesday afternoon when it was determined she was "too pretty" for school. Pepper Fling, 16, was whispering to a boy in class, then promptly told, "go home and don't come back," by her teacher. "She's very pretty and maybe a little too popular," the principal, Ridge Webster explained later. "It was just too disruptive."

SNORING NEIGHBOR IS HERO

A man who snores too loudly is a hero in his own town, especially to his neighbor. Gab Frawley, 48, of Cupboard, Pennsylvania, was snoring "very loudly" early Friday morning, and woke up his neighbor. The neighbor then noticed his own house was on fire. "I got out just in time," the neighbor, Vern Grimmick, 63, said. "Two minutes later, I would've been a hunk of charcoal. Gab's a hero, that's all I can say."

Family Finds Bible in Holiday Turkey

A FAMILY SITTING down to Thanksgiving Dinner was surprised to find a Christian Bible sitting in the stomach of their six-pound turkey dinner. "I was carving real hard, when all of a sudden I saw it," Kell Blent, 38, of Fester, Utah said. "It was sort of a damned miracle," he said. "For us, of course — not the turkey.

Giant Crab Invades House

BY EB TYDE

An uninvited guest entered a Rooster City man's house early Sunday morning. Spleen Geller, 42, said a giant fiddler crab crawled into the living room of his beachfront home, "stayed a while, maybe an hour" then turned around and left. "It seemed like he was looking for something, something real specific, but didn't find it," Geller said. "Like his wife, or girlfriend maybe."

Man Spends Night in Trunk

By Mike Muffley

A LEMMING MAN travelling alone on Interstate 30 last Friday spent the night in his car — in the trunk. Kyle Grest, 53, was changing a flat, when he stumbled on the spare and fell backward, into his trunk. "Somehow the damn thing closed down on me," Grest said. "It was dark in there, and lonely, but luckily not cold. Good thing it was summer."

Chicken Acts Like Pig

Sledge Brewster owns an ordinary chicken — which acts like a pig. "I don't get it," Brewster, 67, of Bluff Bay, Georgia. said. "Porkie looks like an ordinary chicken, but hangs out with the pigs. He rolls around in the sty, gets dirty, and even oinks sometimes, usually when he's sore." He added, "They like him too — I mean the pigs.

Elkton Man Succumbs in Tree

By Shank Harper

Homer Pipps, 90, was pruning branches in his backyard, when he suffered a massive heart attack and died. "He didn't drop but sort of fell forward off his ladder, and got wedged," Marley Ferkus, a longtime neighbor and friend, said. "I'll miss the man. I really will."

SOLAR ECLIPSE IN BATHROOM

A MAN BRUSHING his teeth in Dot City last Monday experienced a rare full solar eclipse when his electric toothbrush briefly blocked out the sun's rays streaming through the window, forming a corona and shadow on the opposite wall. "It was really weird," Mal Leppers, 33, a sixth-grade teacher said, recalling the incident. "A solar eclipse, in my own bathroom!"

Dinosaur Found in Bakery

By Bill Wzczcki

THE REMAINS OF A prehistoric dinosaur were discovered in Fern's Bakery on Highland Street. The reptile's skeleton was found in the cupcake showcase by an employee, Dot McCann, Thursday evening after the bakery had closed. "This is a highly unusual discovery," Sarge Flanagan, a science teacher at Mundy Elementary said soon after hearing about it. "Allosaurus dates from the late Jurassic period, around 145 million years ago. How it ended up in Fern's is anyone's guess."

ive's a lot better.

TV Star Stops at Light

Eb Krindle, who played
the wacky but loveable
plumber on TV's "Meet
The Neighbors", was
seen stopping briefly
at the traffic light in
downtown Oil City last
Wednesday afternoon.
Krindle, 87, a retired
real estate salesman,
had a brief career in
Hollywood in the early
1950's before becoming
a business executive
and plumbing parts
industry spokesman.

SHOE WINS

About the Author

Marc Berlin is an author, actor, filmmaker, and satirist. When not writing, he takes long walks in the woods and cranberry bogs near his home in eastern Massachusetts. His website is at: www.marcberlin.net

Also by Marc Berlin
"The Skeptic's Handbook"

CPSIA information can be obtained
at www.ICGtesting.com
Printed in the USA
LVIW010038280812
296241LV00001B